Hazel Eyes

Danielle Walker

ISBN: 0-9914124-4-3
ISBN-13: 978-0-9914124-4-0

YJLM Publishing House
www.yjlm13productions.com

Printed in the United States of America

ISBN: 0-9914124-4-3

Hazel Eyes

Danielle Walker

CONTENTS

ACKNOWLEDGEMENTS

I want to first give honor to God who is the head of my life and I want to thank him for his continuous favor upon me, which enables me to continue to do what I am passionate about. I want to thank all of my fans who continuously support my work and consistently check in on me to see when the next novel is scheduled to be published. You mean the world to me and without you guys, my story would never be heard. I want to send a special thanks to my grandmother Altha Dean Holloman for always being the first to read my work and giving me her honest opinion. You don't know how much I value you, even though I have a hard way of expressing my gratitude.

I also would like to thank Willie (Will-A-Fool-Muzik) Byrd for your constant encouragement every time I speak with you about my project. You just don't know how grateful I am to have you on my support team. And of course I can't forget Willie Hunter another member of the (Will-A-Fool-Muzik) team. You have been a constant encouragement since the first day we met. And I want to thank you for always taking time out of your busy schedule to come and meet with me to go over any and everything that I have mapped out or have scheduled for an upcoming event. Your blind faith in me is a true blessing from God and I deeply appreciate you and your continuous support. You are heaven sent and a star in my eyes.

Last but not least, I would like to thank Anthony (Ant-Da-Man) Matthews for just always being there for me as my friend. No matter what you may have going on in life I can always count on you to include me and give me a platform to show case my work at your events every chance you get. I have yet to find a friend like you and I wouldn't dare trade you for the world.

Danielle Walker

SURVIVAL OF THE FITTEST

There had never been a more beautiful summer afternoon in the history of mankind, at least through Tamera's eyes. The sun was shining, the squirrels were fighting, and she had twenty more minutes before her summer break officially kicked off. There was nothing like a summer vacation with the people you've spent your entire freshman year of high school with. One minute before the bell sounded, Tami looked up and saw Mo waving hysterically at her outside her homeroom window. Excited, she threw her index finger up to signal her anxious friend to wait but then the bell of freedom rang.

"Class is dismissed!" Mrs. Powell announced to her anxious students who were eager to kick off their summer fun. "Yes!" Monique shouted as she aggressively pushed through the exiting crowd of students to help her best friend pack. "Why aren't you ready?" She asked, while stuffing the last of Tamera's pencils in her purse. "You're the only person in the whole building that brought a book bag to school today!" Shaking her head as she bent to pick the pencil up that was rolling down the aisle.

"Because...", giggling as she watched Mo move as if she had drunk a full pot of coffee that morning. "I needed something to carry as a decoy, so I could sell the rest of my snacks."

"Well, did you make anything?"

"Of course I did…" Guiding her friend down the deserted hall. "You didn't see all that change at the bottom of my bag?" Sashaying through the glass doors of the back entrance.

"Yeah, I saw it." Trailing her out the door. "You gon' let me hold something right?" Starring at Tami with a devious smile on her face.

"Let me flip it first and then I'll see what I can do."

"Cool." Reassured she was going to get a piece of the pot.

As the girls boarded their bus. Tami was distracted by her boyfriend at the time who was leaning over one of the seats flirting with the new chick on the block. Being the woman that she was, Tami didn't believe in chasing no man. She'd just replaced them. And by the looks of things, she had a new admirer of her own.

"Damn, Tami!" Monique blurted. "Ain't that Sean over there flirting with Ke-Ke?" Giving Tami the 'what the heck are you going to do about it' look.

"Yeah." She replied nonchalantly. "I see him over there." Calmly placing her book bag on the seat nearest the window.

"So, what are you going to do about it?" Ready for the 'war' signal.

"Let him have his fun," crossing her legs with grace. "And do me from here on out." Placing her shades on her face.

"What!" Confused on why Tami didn't want to defend her honor, or the relationship she and Sean had for the past six months at least. "Couldn't be me!" She argued. "If I saw Jarmal hanging all over some random." Turning to peer out the window to see if she could spot her boo in the crowd. "My family would have to come and identify my body. Because it's going to be a standoff between me and the feds, after I take him and his hussy down for playing around with my emotions." She advised as she snapped her finger.

Tami just laughed at the thought of Monique being on the six o'clock evening news, surrounded by the APD. But, the sad part about it, she knew Mo was more than capable of pulling it all off.

Usually when school let out, Tami and Mo would go home to change clothes and get ready to head out for their girls day out. But, since Tami was low on product. She needed to go re-up. Because Tami and Mo were best friends. Whenever she would go see Quinton, Mo would be by her side as her right hand girl. It's hard to come by a loyal friend nowadays. But, it's even harder to find someone that is willing to ride, no questions asked. Especially when you're living your life in the fast lane.

"Tamera."

"Yeah."

"What we doing after we leave Quint house?"

"Well, my brother in town for a few days. So, I had planned on spending the weekend with him, before he headed back on the road again."

"Oh…" Looking down at her watch.

"Why?"

"Oh, nothing." She stated nonchalantly. "I wanted to hit up Jr's place to see if I could find me an outfit for this event Jarmal taking me to tomorrow and swing by 'Pamper Me Beauty' for some jewelry as well."

"Is that the guy that created 'First Verse Apparel'?

"Yeah, you know him?"

"Not really, but I've run across a few of his pieces in passing." Impressed by how connected Mo was. "I must admit, he really has some unique items. And the quality is impeccable as well. I haven't seen threads like that since the 90's." She laughed.

"I know, that's why I shop with him."

"Oh, well…" Grabbing her backpack once she realized they were pulling close to Quinton's stop. "Let me see what Arnez going to do and if he ain't got nothing planned. I'll come do a little shopping with you as well. I could use a new shirt or two."

"Alright."

Reminiscing on her past, Tami couldn't believe that out of all the people in the world. Mo would be the one that messed her over. They had been through hell and high water with one another. As she sat tied down like a mental patient being restrained so they couldn't harm themselves, to a cold, wooden, prickly, old chair, that sat in the middle of the dark and gloomy room, in the far end of Bobby's house. She remembered the day she committed her first murder and got away with it. With the help of her supposed best friend.

"Back so soon," Quinton greeted the girls as he stepped aside to allow them access. "What can I do for you ladies on this beautiful summer afternoon?" Twitching, which was a side effect from using one of the products he housed.

"Nothing much." Tami replied. "We just stopped by to re-up real quick." Keeping her tone firm and steady. "I'm running a little low and I have a meeting later this evening."

Even though, Quinton did business with Tami. He frequently, on occasion, forgot where to draw the line between business and pleasure. Usually Tamera would drop by his place alone after school some days, but ever since Quint tried to force himself on her one day while he was high, she didn't trust him enough to come alone anymore. And with a loyal customer base and Quinton being the only dealer with a pure supply at a sensible price, Tamera didn't have no other choice except to keep shopping with him.

"Well, I have some good news and some bad news." Quinton says, bolting the door behind himself. "The good news is I just saved a bunch of money by switching my vehicle over to Geico." Sliding his right hand down the rear of his pants to grab the G-lock he had tucked away. "And, the bad news is," waving the gun around in the air to assist with finishing his statement. "Ain't no transactions being made, until one of y'all drain my sack," Pulling the clip back to verify that the gun was undoubtedly loaded.

Monique was terrified. She had never been held up at gunpoint before, nor, has she ever been threatened with rape. She didn't know what to do or how she was going to get herself out of this sticky situation. Just another innocent bystander in the wrong place at the wrong time. Tami on the other hand, wasn't going down without a fight. Little did Quinton know, she came prepared and was ready for war. She knew the day would come when she was going to have to fight him off, but she regretted it having to be the day when Mo came along with her.

"So, who's it going to be?" He asked, using the tip of his pistol to scratch his head. Neither of the girls said a word. They continued to remain quiet and watched their predator as he stood nonchalantly as if it didn't matter to him one way or the other who did it, as long as it got done. "I'll tell you what," coming up with a solution to solve their ever present dilemma. "How about you start getting undressed," pointing to Tamera. "And, you!" Glancing at Mo. "New kid on the block," turning his back as he headed towards the nearest comforter. "Follow me."

Before Quinton had a chance to turn back around, Tami had shot him in the back of his head execution style. Mo screamed simultaneously as she watched his body fall in what seemed like slow motion, before her eyes. The sight was so devastating to them both, because a huge chunk of his head was blown away from the impact. In shock, both girls hesitated for a few seconds, one with her eyes wide open and the other breathing heavily as if she'd just finished running a five mile marathon.

"What are we going to do?" Monique asked, still looking down at Quinton's stiff corpse.

"I don't know." Tami replied, pacing back and forth, rubbing her forehead.

"Do you think someone heard the shot?" Panicking at the thought of possibly facing jail time for being an accomplice to murder. "I can't afford to go to jail right now," she whined. "I'm too young to die!" Wiping the tears that began to form in her eyes. "What am I going to tell my mom?" she cried. "The embarrassment she'll go through over this." Continuing to panic. "Do you know what they do to pretty girls like us in jail?" Thinking of the consequences of their actions.

Still pacing back and forth, Tami tuned out everything Mo was saying so she could possibly think of something to get them out of this mess she got them in. She never intended on killing Quinton. Things just got out of hand. She wasn't going to sit back and let him violate her again, just because he decided to get high and needed a nut. She didn't get down like that and she definitely wasn't going to allow him to take advantage of her friend either. If it wasn't for her Mo wouldn't be in the predicament that they were in now. And she was going to protect them both by any means necessary.

'Maybe I should've shot him in the leg or something'. Debating with herself subconsciously as she continued to fret secretly. 'He always on that fuck shit, man!' Pushing her hair back from out her face. 'Why he just can't handle business without using his dick to think.' She continued. 'Fuck it, we got to get up out of here.' Tossing the gun on the floor.

"Help me straighten up a bit," she instructed.

"Do you think someone heard us?" Mo asked while scanning the area.

"Naw…" Lying to insure Mo helped her clean and stop freaking out. "All we have to do is make it seem like a deal gone wrong." Tossing some money on the floor. "And we good." Using her jacket to wipe the gun down. "Empty some of this weed on the table over there." Grabbing a pound of weed from his dish washer.

"Okay," Mo Doing as she was told.

While the girls continued to manipulate the crime scene. Neither one of them noticed Quinton's business associate, peering at them through the front window. He recognized Mo instantly, because he knew her brother from some old beef they had coming up on the block. And he knew Tami, because she was a regular dealer that bought from Quint.

"Let's go," Tami says, picking up her book bag from off the floor. "We taking the back door." Pulling her jacket out once more to assist with turning the door knob. "From this day forward. We will never speak of this ever again. You got me?"

"Got it." Anxious to get this day over and wake up from the nightmare.

Months had passed since the death of Quinton Sky, and the memory haunted Mo every night since. She started drinking her sorrows away and smoking her thoughts away, as well. Every day was a nightmare for her, because she felt like everyone knew and all eyes were on her. But, karma has its way of getting back around to you. Even though, Tami shot Quinton in self-defense. The dude that saw them didn't know that was the case. So, he sought revenge. A life for a life. Unfortunately, Mo was the victim of the retaliation.

One Saturday evening Bobby had left out to handle a few things and Mo was asleep in bed. A red dolo monte carlo pulled up in front of their home and let off a dozen rounds. At the time of the incident, Monique's mom was in the kitchen preparing dinner, and her eldest brother was sitting on the porch. Nothing could have prepared her for the sight she had awoken to. And she regretted the fact that she survived by rolling on the floor. From that day forward, Bobby and Mo had been looking for the guy that turned their lives upside down. And she had a vendetta against Tami for bringing her in this mess in the first place.

'I have to get out of here.' Tami thought as she continued to look around the dark room. Bobby had left her there for dead and he wasn't coming back. It was either live or die trying. Survive or die. And at that moment, Tami chose life.

Unsure of what level she was on, Tami was still willing to take the risk. Inching her chair slowly to the window, she steadily eased her back facing it, so her landing wouldn't be too harsh. Falling out a window faced forward while tied to a chair, is not an ideal landing. But, by the chair being made of wood, landing on it could potentially cause it to break and she'd be free. The only thing that caused her to continue to hesitate, was the thought of how high she possibly could be. Regardless, there was no time for chickening out. What's done is done and this needed to be done.

Taking a deep breath to prepare herself mentally and physically for the shock of her life, Tami used all the force she could muscle up to launch herself out the window. Surprisingly, the window was about a good forty inches from the ground. The ironic part about her situation was the fact that the chair didn't break. She was still bound and it felt as though her right arm had broken. So not only was she still trapped, but she was in excruciating pain, as well. Lying face up on the side of Bobby's house with no way to scream because her mouth was taped shut. 'Why me!' She thought.

Even though, Tami was still in a compromising position. She still saw the bright light at the end of the tunnel. At least she wasn't still trapped in the house where no one would ever find her. And when the sun rinse, hopefully someone would discover her lying there. Now her only concern was making it through the night, without mother nature and her critters attacking her.

Danielle Walker

AT LAST

Refusing to get out of bed. Cameron continued to ignore all texts, calls, and alarms her phone was singing. Stuck in a paralyzed daze, she couldn't shake the fear of what Bobby had in store for her. The one thing that bothered her the most about the note was the part where he stated he was going to get her. What the heck did she do for him to want to bring harm towards her. Rising up out of bed finally, Cameron crept down the hall to allow Bear to relieve himself. Cracking the front door, she let him run free and she immediately shut it back, leaving him out there on his own.

"That crazy bastard ain't getting me just yet." She reassured herself. "He's going to have to work to get to me." Latching the chain and bolting the master lock. "Dang, I'm hungry." Rubbing her aching tommy. "I guess I do have a little time to whip something up," rubbing her hands across her face to wipe the sleep away.

As Cameron walked to her refrigerator, she heard her pup barking aggressively and whimpering. Feeling the need to investigate with her new threat lurking around next door, she grabbed the closest frying pan and walked out on the porch.

"Bear!" She called out for him. "Poo-b, come to mommy!" Awaiting her baby to come rushing toward her. But to her surprise, he didn't come.

13

Bear continued to bark and whine as if he was trying to get her attention. "Please don't let my puppy be hurt!" She cried.

Walking down the steps of her porch, Cameron followed the sound of her frantic dog until she saw him standing beside a woman tied to a chair lying on the ground.

"Oh my god…" She whispered in shock as the pan fell to the ground and hit her toe on its way down. "SHIT!" She shouted as she hopped around in a circle. "FUCK!" She yelled while bending down to check for blood. "Get over here!" She demanded, but he didn't obey.

Cameron didn't know what to do. Here was a woman lying on the side of her home, who obviously came out of Bobby's window. Tied to a chair and was apparently bruised up from a beating. She didn't know whether to leave the lady there or help. But one things for sure, she really, really, really didn't want to get involved. So she decided to go, until the nameless stranger made eye contact.

"Shoot!" says Cameron, stomping her foot on the ground. "You just had to be alive didn't you," moving closer to assist with untying the damsel.

When Cameron pulled the tape from Tami's mouth. Tami released a deep breath and started crying. Even though, she was in so much pain, she was still relieved to be free. Tami never thought she would make it out of that house alive and she did. She didn't say anything initially to Cameron as she helped her in the house. But, she later said thank you once she was sitting on the big comfy couch in Cameron's living room.

"I owe you my life." Tami cried as she gulped down a big ounce of spit. "How can I ever repay you?"

"Look lady." Cameron says, while standing in front of her with her hands on her hips. "You don't owe me anything. I just want you out of my house as if nothing ever happened." Trying to redirect her attention to the front door.

"But, you just saved my life." Confused on why this lady was being so heartless to her under her current circumstances. "Whatever you need or want as payment, just state it and I can get it for you."

Before Cameron continued her quest of getting this lady out of her house, she wanted to pluck a little information out of her first. *'And who is she to say that she can give me whatever I want.'* Cameron thought. *'She ain't famous, because I would've seen her on tv or something. And they didn't do any missing persons announcements either.'* Rubbing her chin. *'Let me see.'*

"Who are you?" she asked in an inconsiderate manner.

"My name is Tamera King." Gripping her fractured arm in an attempt to reduce the pain.

'Tamera is it.' Cameron thought to herself as she continued to stare. "And, why were you tied to a chair again?" Ignoring the fact that it would be courteous to offer Tami a Tylenol to assist with her pain relief. But the side effects would be drowsiness and sleep, and Cameron made it clear her company wasn't welcomed.

"It's a long story." Shifting to the right to get a glimpse of Bobby's driveway to see if he made it back yet.

"Well, I know by you telling me what happened would put me in a compromising position. But, damn that! If it wasn't for me and my dog, you'd still be a baking potato. So, cut the crap and spill it!" Folding her arms as she became more irritated with the thought of not knowing what she had gotten herself into.

Looking at the expression of aggravation on Cameron's face, made Tami realize she wasn't going to ease up off the obvious, until she told her everything she wanted know. And if she planned on getting herself nursed back to health, without having to admit herself into the hospital, then, she had no other choice but to tell the truth. Explaining how she'd gotten herself in this predicament wasn't the issue. The problem was Cameron finding out why it started in the first place, that brought about Tamera's concern. How would she react? Would she throw her out? Would she call the police? Was she in cohorts with Bobby and this was a confession attempt? Could she be trusted? Can anyone be trusted? Tami didn't know what to think, but she knew what had to be done. She needed an ally. And what better way to seek revenge, than to have the closest person to your enemy literally on your side.

"I kidnapped his sister initially and he retaliated after her release."
Gasping for air as she threw her hands over her mouth. Cameron couldn't believe the words that were coming out of Tamera's mouth. Did she hear what she thought she'd heard, or are her ears playing tricks on her. What had she gotten herself entangled in?

But, was she really that surprised about her findings? Because deep down she knew Bobby was up to no good when they first met. Secondly, Tami looked like the type of woman to walk on the wild side occasionally. She was average height, light skinned, and although she had a soft girly demeanor, her body was still covered in tattoos from shoulder to wrist. Your typical good girl gone homicidal maniac kind of look.

"Dag…" Looking Tami straight in her eyes. "What did she do?" Surprised by her reaction, Tami continued to fill Cameron in on the details of why she'd taken Mo in the first place.

"The streets been talking and I've been catching wind of Mo stating you're responsible for the death of her mom and brother." Jasmine stated as she curled Tamera's hair.

"What!" Lifting her head to get a glance at Jasmine in the mirror.

"Yeah…" Rotating her comb and curling iron around her hand as she twirled a portion of Tamera's hair into a perfect circle. "She said if it wasn't

16

for you none of what happened would've happened." Combing through her bangs.

"What else have you heard?" Furious at the thought of Mo going around the neighborhood blabbing about what went down at Quint's house. Rule number one is to never snitch, no matter what the circumstances are. But don't get it twisted, Tami felt bad for what happened to Monique's family, and she was more than willing to help get the guy that did this to them. But, what help would she be if Mo was out spilling over like a sink full of water.

"A few girls that came through the shop the other day was talking about it. And I heard one of them say she was going to put you six feet under."

Realizing how real things were getting, Tamera thought to beat her to the punch. She planned to convince Mo to come over to her crib. And as soon as she walks in, she'd knock her unconscious before she could turn around.

"Bet…" Tami says, making herself more comfortable in her seat. "What's your calendar availability looking like so we can schedule my next appointment?"

"Well…" Spraying oil sheen on her hair to give it a nice shine. "This is my last week taking clients."

"Say what!" Turning to face her.

"Yeah girl, I thought you knew." Snatching the apron from around Tami's shoulders. "I start school next week."

"School!" Unsure if she should be happy or pissed at her friends sudden departure. "I mean, I'm excited that you're trying to better yourself and all." Tami states, while counting out sixty dollars from the wad of cash she pulled from her bra. "But, who's going to do my hair from here on out if you leave?"

"You can still come to the shop, my mom will be here." Recounting the money she received. "This was just a source of income while I was in high school, because my mama wanted me to focus. And I could set my own schedule here as well."

"Have you decided where you were going to attend school yet?"

"Silverman."

"Where's that?"

"In Hot-Lanta."

"Atlanta!" Curious of why she's deciding to move so far away. "If you like it, I love it. And I wish you the best."

"Thank you. I'll see you around when I come back for summer vacation."

"Cool."

"But my friend never returned and I never saw her again." Tami stated as her eyes began to well again.

'Damn...' Cameron said to herself as she watched this complete stranger unfold before her eyes on her living room love seat. '*Should I offer her my help?*' She thought.

"Well..." Coming back to the reality of the situation at hand. "I'm sorry all of these unfortunate events keep happening to you, maybe you're just an unlucky individual, but you have to go." Cameron says, heading towards the door. "I don't want no part in what you got going on. I have my own demons to deal with right now." Using her arm to guide Tamera out the door. "Hold on." Grabbing the half empty bottle of Tylenol off the table. "Take these with you. You may need them." Placing the bottle in her hand. "God's speed."

After having the door slammed in her face, Tami took hold of her pride and proceeded down the driveway. At that moment, there was nothing anyone could do or say to steal the relief of freedom she felt as the sun shined down on her skin and the wind blew through her hair. Revenge was running threw her mind, but this time around, she figured she'd bury the grudge.

Danielle Walker

NOWHERE TO RUN

After walking around in la, la land for the past three days, Shelly didn't know what to do or what to say about the text message she received from Paul. When Michael questioned her about what happened, she played it off by stating she was feeling lightheaded and lost her balance. She didn't want to stir up anymore drama between them two, and knowing Shelly had always been honest with him in the past. Michael never questioned the response she'd given. Never in a million years, did she think Paul, of all people, would contact her and try to be a part of their, now teenage daughter's life.

"Out of all these years he'd let pass him by." Shaking her head as she gazed at the home she had created with her now fiancé Michael, from the seat of her brand new Cadillac Deville. "He better have a damn good excuse for popping up this time around." Turning the metallic key in the ignition. "Something's got to give, real talk."

Debra had been cleaning up the house all morning. So when Shelly came walking through the front door, she was relieved to take a much needed break. Running her vacuum over the last patch of unkempt carpet underneath the coffee table, she eagerly used her foot to power off the machine, and flopped down on the love seat nearest the door.

"Woo…" Pulling an old worn out handkerchief from her apron to wipe the sweat from her forehead. "Child… I ain't never been so happy to see anybody walk through that front door, as I am right about now." Swinging the rag back and forth to conduct a small breeze. "What brings you on this side of town today? Usually you'd call and let me know you're coming." Tilting her head back with her eyes closed, as she shifted her dentures in place with her tongue.

Coincidentally, Shelly said nothing. Not one peep, not even a mumble of a sentence in response. She stood in the middle of her mother's foyer, gazed at the clock on the wall, and dropped everything she had in the floor. Lost in the sauce, and needing a way of escape.

"Gal!" Pissed, because she had just got finished mopping the entire house. And here comes Shelly, creating a mess on her Mr. Clean and Pine Sol tiles. "What the heck done got into you!" Throwing the hanky on the floor. Getting ready to tackle Shelly as if she was a defensive lineman guarding the end zone. "I don't know what you got going on, but all I know you better get that mess up off my floor and act like you got some darn sense up in here. Or it's going to be me and you sister!"

"I'm sorry mama." She apologizes in a meek tone emotionlessly, with no sense of urgency.

"What done got into you, child?" Noticing her daughter looked as if she had seen a ghost. "Is everything alright with my grandson?" Easing back down on the sofa. "Did you and that boy have a disagreement or something?" Reaching for her hanky. "I knew something was up with him. He smiles too much and is too quiet if you ask me." Wiping her face once again. "You have to keep your eye on people like that."

"It ain't got nothing to do with either of them mama." Taking a seat next to Debra with a big sigh of relief.

"Well, what is it then child? I don't have time to play these guessing games with you today honey. I have clothes I need to finish folding and put up, you hear."

"It's just, if it ain't one thing it's another." She cried.

"Awe, what's wrong baby?" Leaning over to embrace Shelly as she continued to cry.

"It's like..." Trying to get a grip over her tears. "Once I get out of one mess, another pile is waiting on my other foot to step in it." Pouring her heart out in her mother's arms.

"Look baby, I know it's been rough around here lately. But, you'll pull through it." Rocking her side to side. "I'm pretty sure whatever it is this time, ain't as bad as you're making it seem."

"First it was the accident, then Bernard and all his drama. I lost my best friend and now I don't have nobody to talk to. I almost got killed over some freaking cookies and now this b.s!" Sitting up as she wiped her face.

"I'm not quite understanding what it is you're trying to say." Nervous about finding out what obstacle they are having to face after all they've been through in the past.

"Paul wants to see Nette."

Suddenly, for the first time in sixty-one years. Debra was speechless. Nineteen years had come and gone, like a breeze with no real hardship. And, now the one man that can come and flip their whole world upside down had arrived. Now that the restraining order has expired, they have no right to keep him away from his daughter.

"I love you so much baby girl." Paul says, rubbing his hands around her apple bottom.

"I love you too daddy long stroke." She giggled.

"Prove it..."

Pulling him on top of her, Shelly removed the condom that protected his body part from her tenderness and divided her legs. *'I'm ready.'* She whispered as she anticipated his embrace. The touch of his skin against hers was so erotic that Shelly lost all focus on his rhythm and concentrated more on the thought of his penis gliding in and out of her vaginal opening. Even though the session lasted for seven minutes, it felt like the best seven minutes either one of them had ever experienced in their entire lives.

"How does it feel?" He asked, looking down over her as he continued to stroke. But Shelly said nothing. She was lost in her thoughts and the enjoyment of the sensation. "I'm about to nut." He warned as he released his treasure in her box and collapsed on the side of her.

Several days had passed when Shelly noticed she had missed her period. Remembering the session she had the other night at Paul's raised some suspicion, so she went to the doctors for a checkup.

"How could you do this to me!" She cried. "I'm not ready to be a mother! Let alone be stuck with you for the rest of my life!"

"What the fuck are you talking about? Don't be calling my phone with all that bullshit!" Paul replied, confused.

"I'm pregnant Paul! And it's your baby!"

"Fuck you mean, you pregnant! It ain't my fucking kid!" He denied as he paced back and forth in his bedroom.

"But, I ain't been with nobody else!" She welled. "You were my first!"

"You a got damn lie! You know what, I ain't feeling your vibes right now. You can miss me with all this fuckery right here. You have three choices." He advised. "Either get an abortion, raise it without me, or I'll come beat it out of you." Rubbing his hand across his head. "Ain't no way in hell I'm finna be tied down to no ho!" He shouted. "As a matter of fact, I'm on the way!"

Unsure of what Paul could want now after all of these years. Debra picked up her hanky and stood from the sofa and took one last look at her distraught daughter.

"The only thing I can suggest you do, is tell her before it's too late," Debra says, using the rag to wipe her face once more. "With everything that has been taking place these past couple of years, I'm not all that surprised he decided to pop up." Looking off into the abyss. "I've grown tired of keeping this secret from that child anyway and the way Candice walking around here as if she'd done lost her damn mind since she found out, it'll only be a matter of time before Nette knows." Debra remarks as she is heading out the room. "What's done in the dark always come to the light. Even though our intentions of doing what we did were in the right place, now it's high time for us to pay the piper."

Left alone with her thoughts, Shelly couldn't fathom why all of this was happening to her. Instead of continuing to frustrate herself with past demons she couldn't contain any longer, she decided to come up with a plan on how she was going to keep Paul away for good.

With his sweaty palms gripping the steering wheel, Bobby bolted through the evening traffic on highway 285 as he continued his desperate attempt to remain a free man. Several miles away from his home, he had lost the last tail on his car, when he turned down the side alley the Feds had failed to cover. Realizing his final destination was nearly ten minutes away, he didn't feel relief, because he knew at any given moment a squad car could spot him and take him down.

"Damn it!" Slamming his hand on the steering wheel. He could see the flashing lights from the highway that surrounded the dock where the boat was parked. "Fuck!" He shouted, as he continued to drive pass the exit, watching the twins standing in the middle of the road with their arms in the air.

Message: The boat's been compromised. They got the twins. Where are you? He texted.

"I'm on 5th Ave, meet me at the Spot." The messenger replies.

Making his way to 5th Ave, Bobby wondered why Paul wasn't at the dock himself. He was the one who came up with the plan, yet, he's the only one who wasn't there or heading in that direction at the time he set for everyone to meet. With everything falling apart, Bobby didn't know whether to trust him or not. But, whatever excuse he may have for not being there, better be a darn good one. If not, he was prepared to do what was necessary to get rid of the rat.

'What's up!' Bobby questioned intensely leaving the car door open. "You were supposed to be at the dock! What's good fam?" Banging his chest before he threw his arms in the air. Approaching Paul, who was posted up against his car, smoking a cigarette. "What's up!"

But, Paul said nothing. He stood there with his head hung low, while he took one last pull from his addiction and tossed it on the ground. He slowly eased his head up as he released the fumes and stared Bobby in the eyes.

"I couldn't leave."

"Nigga! What you mean you couldn't leave!" Punching his fist out of anger, imagining it was Paul's face.

"I couldn't do it," Paul answered nonchalantly.

"You couldn't do what?" Bobby yelled, unsure of the emotions he's experiencing right about now. Here stands his best friend in the whole wide world, telling him to his face that he couldn't leave the country and they could be possibly facing life in jail, in a manner as if he's had an epiphany or something. "See I need you to give me a little bit more than what you're giving me right now, because I just got chased by the cops! And the one

26

place that YOU told us to meet you at!" Screams Bobby, pacing back and forth. "Is swarming with badges and everyone was there except you!" Pointing his finger in Paul's direction. "So excuse me if I seem a little fucked up right now. Naw fuck that!" Now standing him face to face. "What's good G?"

"I got to see her." Paul replies as tears began to fall.

At that moment Bobby knew. He knew there was nothing that could change Paul's mind about getting the heck out of dodge, after that statement was made. He had waited eighteen years for the day he'd finally get to meet his daughter, and now that the restraining order had been lifted he was going to do just that.

"When did you decide this?" Bobby asks, releasing his anger.

"After I left your crib." Staring off in the dark abyss, Paul attempts to maintain his composure. "I sent Shell a text."

"What she say?" Leaning up against the car, next to Paul.

"She didn't respond, but I got to meet my lil shorty, man." Looking back at his friend.

"I feel you dog. But this ain't the time. We hot right now."

"Don't you think I know that." He agreed. "But we don't know how this thing is going to play out. The way I see it we got three options."

"And what's that?" Confused on what the third choice might be, being he could only think of two.

"One, we get away scott free."

"Yeah." Nodding in agreement. "And that's the one I'm banking on."

"Two, we get caught and go to jail." Using his fingers as markers.

"I thought about that, but the plan is to avoid the cell by any means."

"And three, we die trying."

Never considering death being on the table, Bobby didn't have anything else to say after he realized this was the reality they were facing now. He didn't want to go to jail and he for damn sure wasn't ready to die. But, he knew no matter what he decided to do. His fate was sealed the night they kidnapped Tami.

"So what's it going to be?" Bobby asks.

"Let's go meet my daughter."

FOREVER MAYBE

The big day had finally come and Stephanie couldn't be more nauseous. As she stood in the mirror and admired herself in the all-white Vera Wang she'd spent the majority of her retirement savings on. She still continued to battle with her conscious as to whether or not she was making the right decision. Things hadn't been the same between her and Rico since the night he came back home. And honestly, the only thing that was keeping her in the church was the fact that she was twenty-seven, never married, and she didn't want to disappoint her family.

"Ms. Reed." One of the ushers called out to her from the other side of the door.

"Yes!" She replies as she takes one last look at herself in the mirror and exhale.

"The groom is awaiting you." She whispers.

"I'm on the way." Forcing a smile on her face to hide her guilt of wanting to flee.

'As I pour this glass of wine. I hope it helps me express these thoughts of mine... I don't think I ever felt the way I feel for you girl. So I'm turning these lights down and I'm telling you right now... I don't think I ever, ever really told you, how much I need you. I need you more than my next breath.' Played in the background as everyone

29

turned and saw the bride standing at the entrance of the sanctuary. At that moment, every eye in the building was filled with tears. Never had any of her guest laid eyes on a more stunning bride, until today. She truly was a dream.

As her father walked beside her down the aisle, she felt him grip her left hand as if he never wanted to let her go. By the time she had met her groom, perspiration was plastered all over her forehead. Yet, she smiled anyway.

While the reverend was giving his matrimonial speech. The only thing that was racing through Ricardo's mind, was the image of the woman with the hazel eyes. The excitement he felt in his heart when he remembered her smile caused him to feel as if he was suffocating, as he watched the lips of the pastor continue to mumble his fate. After having a complete out of body experience, his day dream was over as soon as the pastor asked him. *'And do you take Stephanie Reed to be your lawfully wedded wife? To have and to hold, through sickness and health, for better and for worse, till death do you both part?"*

"I can't…"

(Gasps… "What…" Whispers…)

You could only imagine the look of surprise on everyone's face after they've heard Ricardo's objection.

"I can't marry you Step." Facing her with pity in his eyes. "I love you, I do. But, I can't commit to forever."

"Awe, hell naw!" Someone shouted from the back pew. "Let's get this fool!"

Ring, ring, ring… Ring, ring, ring… **You have reached the voicemail of Arnez Jenkins. Right now Arnez Jenkins, is not able to take your call right now. Please leave a message at the sound of the tone. *Beep***

"Nez, this Tami." She frantically whispered in the receiver. "I messed up, so I'm hoping you've skipped town like we agreed." Looking around the telephone booth to see if anyone had followed her. "I don't have a way for you to contact me at the moment, but I'm going to be at the 'Spot' in two hours. Send someone to come pick me up if you can."

Placing the phone back down on the post, Tami wiped the tears from her cheeks and started down the breezeway. It had been years since she'd had the luxury of taking a stroll due to always having to watch her back and make sure her money was intact. Today was no different, because she still had people after her. But, it was bittersweet because she actually had a chance to start her life over.

When Bobby kidnapped Tami everyone that knew her knew she was missing, due to all of the news reports that went out in efforts to locate her. But her escaping and the news still hadn't stated she'd been found, it's the dawn of a new day. "I have to get out of here," she stated as she looked over at the old couple sitting on the bench, feeding a group of pigeons that were fighting for a crumb.

Noticing a huge commotion carrying on in front of a church a few blocks ahead. Tami started to make a detour, until she saw a man in a tuxedo, run past her and a small mob that followed. She chuckled for a bit, until she saw the bride come out in tears. It reminded her of all the heartbreak she'd gone through in her past relationships. But, none of them could compare to what this poor woman was experiencing.

"Excuse me."

"Whaattt." Stephanie cried out in a haunting tone.

"I know this may not be the right time or the right place, but it's going to be okay." She reassured her in a compassionate tone. "Don't cry." Attempting to console the stranger. "Whatever he did, God can erase the pain and replace him with someone ten times better."

But Stephanie said nothing. She continued to pour her heart out in the middle of 9th Ave and there was nothing anyone could do or say to change the way she felt. Rico's decision to turn back on his promise to marry her, wasn't the issue. Not even the fact of him waiting to embarrass her in front of both their families and friends, was enough to push her off the edge. The thorn Stephanie couldn't get over that put the icing on the cake, is the amount of money she'd wasted on her dress alone.

Stephanie had been saving and cutting back on her expenses for the past seven years. Ever since the first day Ricardo proposed to her. She had made up in her mind *this was it*. Her chariot had finally come and she wasn't going to be the laughing stock of her family anymore. Or, the butt of her sisters random jokes. Unfortunately, that declaration went down the drain when 'can't' came out of his mouth.

"He can't!" She shouted. "HA!!!" Bursting out in sudden laughter. "Do you drink?"

"Pardon me?" Tami asked, thinking to herself, that the woman had lost her mind.

"I was asking if you drink?" Standing with both hands on her hips.

Tami looked at the torn woman with her puffy red eyes and imagined the shoe being on the other foot. Then, she thought about the emotional roller coaster she'd just got off of. Being trapped in a room not knowing if she was going to ever see the light of day ever again. It didn't take long for her to realize she deserved that drink she was being offered. And to have someone to share it with, was well worth the escape.

"Yes." She answered after clearing her throat. "Yes, I do." With a welcoming smile.

"Well, I've got several bottles of Champagne in the banquet hall paid for, if you care to join me."

"I think I just may take you up on that offer miss lady."

"Haa, haaa!" Shouted Stephanie.

"What's that?" Curiously questioning what's funny.

"You said 'miss'…"

"Ooops, my bad."

Danielle Walker

THE EYE OF THE BEHOLDER

Dawn broke and there had been no updates from Lewis about Tami's where about. The hospital was releasing Arnez and he had never been more anxious to hit the ground running. His overseeing nurse came and dropped off his discharge papers earlier that morning, while Rock was sitting in the waiting room awaiting him to get dressed. Reaching for his blackberry, Arnez noticed the message light was blinking. Thumbing through the missed calls, he went straight to the message center and pressed play. Once he heard his sisters voice, the sensation he felt in his chest was enough to get him readmitted in the ICU if they'd had him attached to a pressure machine. Snatching his cuff links off the table, Arnez rushed through the door and motioned for his friend.

"Tami called me last night." Limping down the hall.

"Word!" Excited to hear the news.

"Yeah, but I just got her message a few minutes ago." Pressing the call button for the elevator.

"What she say?" Rock asked out of curiosity. Concerned for what was about to take place.

"We got to get to the club asap."

"Cool."

When they got down to the parking garage, Arnez sent Lewis a text to let him know where they were going to meet. Nothing was going to stand in the way of him getting to his sister this time. He just hoped she'd be there when he arrived.

After running five miles in efforts of ditching the mob, Rico found himself in between a rock and a hard place. He couldn't go back to the place he once called home, because he ruined that when he left Stephanie standing at the altar. He made the decision not to contact any of his family members, because he wasn't prepared to explain his actions to anyone. Not yet at least. So, he decided to spend the night in his truck. As the sun beamed down on his eyelids and they slowly opened, what Ricardo thought was a dream became his reality, when he realized he was still wearing his tux. Hopping out of his cab, Rico slowly walked over to the diner to order up some morning grub.

"Long night, huh?" The waitress probed as she placed a menu on the table.

"You can say that." Exhaling as he repositioned the place setting in front of him.

"What can I get you to drink?" Pulling out her pencil and notepad.

"Let me start with a coffee, two creamers, and six sugars please." Rubbing his chin as he tried to clear his mind to focus on ordering his meal.

"And how would you like your eggs?"

"Scrambled with cheese. Grits instead of hash browns. Extra crispy waffle and grape jelly, no syrup," he said, handing the menu back to her.

"Coming right up in a jiffy."

Gazing out the window, Rico imagined the magnitude of pain Stephanie was experiencing due to his selfish decision not to go through with the I do's. Why he waited until the day of the wedding to do what he did, baffled him. There was no explanation for his actions and no matter how hard he tried to justify it to himself, nothing could undo the damage he'd done. Living with the fact that he walked out on something that could have potentially been eternal was something he could live with due to the fact that he didn't want it with her. Startled by the footsteps drawing nigh, Rico prepared himself to feast, but to his surprise it was the last person he'd ever expect to see, Mo!

"We have to stop meeting like this." She greeted with a flirtatious smile.

"Wow…" Rico says, in awe of her beauty. Leaning back in the booth as he admired the hazel eyed angel. "Don't you look refreshing this morning," unable to hide his admiration.

"And don't you look like a pile of crap." She chuckled as she sat to join him.

"Cold," he laughed. "Real cold." Clearing his throat. "What brings you in my neck of the woods?" Straightening his wrinkled blazer, as he continued to appreciate her company. "I would've never imagined you being on this side of the bridge."

"And what does that supposed to mean?" Sitting her purse inside the booth to guard from the locals.

"I mean you seem suburban-ish." Shrugging his shoulders. "The fancy type." Serenading *That girl and her fancies* by The Dream.

"Haha…" She snickered. "Perception is a mother." Consuming a huge amount of air. "I'm more like the type of girl you want to chew all of my bubble gum." Exhaling as she took her right hand around her head to grip her flowing ponytail, and rest it on her shoulder.

"See, that right there." Shaking his head. "Is the reason I'm in the predicament I'm in right now."

"And what's that?"

Before Rico could go into the details of what his life had become, the waitress returned with his meal.

"I didn't know you were expecting a guest." Placing the food on the table. "We could have requested something to be prepared for her as well."

"This date wasn't planned." Mo replied. "However, I'll have what he's having."

"Good deal." The waitress says, heading back to the kitchen.

"And you can put it on his tab!" She yelled.

Picking up his fork after saying grace, Rico mixed his grits and eggs and chopped on a nice portion of his waffle.

"Date, huh?" He questioned with sarcasm while chewing.

"Yep." Crossing her legs. "A date."

"And what makes you think this is a date?" Stuffing more food in his mouth as he awaited her response. "I never asked you out."

"Well, you can call it what you want. But, I consider this a date. Since you're single and all." Looking down at her fingernails.

"What makes you think I'm single?" Taking a sip of his coffee.

"Because I was there when you bailed on your fiancé."

Monique had been driving around for hours trying to figure out what she was going to do with her life. Her brother kidnapped the one person she hated and loved at the same time. She wouldn't go back to her old condo because she spotted a SWAT car a few blocks from her home and being as paranoid as she was, she knew they were waiting for her return. The only other place she knew she could go to was the church. Where she could speak with the reverend to seek guidance, before she messed up her sobriety completely.

"Excuse me," says Monique.

"Yes?" The usher answered with a welcoming smile. "Are you here for the bride or the groom?"

"Neither." She replied as she looked around puzzled at the people gathered in the sanctuary. "I'm actually here to see if I could speak with the Pastor."

"Oh, I do apologize about the mix up." She chuckled. "But, Reverend Cole is about to do a matrimony sermon. But, you're welcome to stay until he finishes."

"Ok, I'll wait."

"Good." She smiled. "You can have a seat in the back. I'm pretty sure our guests wouldn't mind you being there at all."

"Thank you."

"Of course, my child."

Sliding into the sanctuary. Monique took a seat next to an elderly man that smelled like he took a bath in Old Spice. Trying to ignore the burning sensation, she placed her attention on the groom that was standing near the pulpit that looked awfully familiar.

"That's him!" She said shockingly to herself as her heart plummeted to her stomach. "I can't believe this." Lost for words.

Watching the bride walk down the aisle made her thirst for cognac heighten. The closer she got to Ricardo, the dryer her mouth became. As Reverend Cole begun the ceremony, the room started to spin and Mo got lightheaded. Before she started suffocating, an instant breeze came rushing by her and that's when she noticed it was Rico running out the church. Unbeknownst to Mo what happened between the bride's walk down the aisle and her own personal panic attack, the groom decided to run out the door. Unsure why, but relieved he did. Mo ran to her car and followed him to the truck stop and she waited. She waited for the opportunity to present itself when she could finally address him.

The shattering of Ricardo's mug caught the attention of every customer in the diner. Every mumble of a conversation was halted, and all eyes were on them.

"Is everything alright?" The waitress asked as she came dashing across the parlor to assist.

"Yes, everything is fine." He reassured. "I do apologize for making such a mess and breaking your glass. I can pay for it when we close my tab." Rising from his seat to help clean up the spill. "I was caught off guard with some shocking information from my date here." Staring at Mo as he addressed the waitress. "But, we're fine now. I promise."

"Ok." Picking up a few pieces of the mug from under the table. "Here's a couple of napkins so you can dry yourself off. And I'll be right back with another fresh cup of coffee for you. And your order as well." Looking over at Mo with a bit of hesitation.

"Thank you." They both thanked with gratitude.

"Why didn't you tell me you were getting married?" She whispered.

"Why didn't you tell me you were at my wedding?" Feeling a bit of tension between the two.

"Why did you run?"

"What does it matter?"

"Why did you run!" Slamming her fist down on the table.

"For you!" Aggressively whispering back as he looked around the restaurant, smiling at onlookers.

"What?" Confused by his response. "What do I have to do with anything?"

"Nothing, just let it go." Placing a napkin in his lap.

"No!" Getting louder. "I want to know why you broke that poor woman's heart. And I want to know now!"

"Can we talk about this later?" Leaning over the table. "When it's less people around speculating what we're discussing."

"No!" Becoming unruly. "You said it has something to do with me and I want to know what!" Crossing her arms.

"Because I want you!" Declaring for the entire room to hear.

"What…" Confused on how he could say something like that. "But you don't even know me." Staring him in the eyes. "We've only met once."

"And that was enough." He admitted. "I fell for you that night and I couldn't shake my feelings." Pushing his plate aside. "I had to see you again and take that chance on the possibility of what if."

Mo was speechless. She had finally bit off more than she could chew. She just stared and glanced at the man that walked out on his future to gamble with a future of happiness with a woman he barely even knew.

"But, what if we aren't compatible?" She asked with compassion in her heart and sympathy in her eyes.

"Well, that's a risk I'm willing to take."

Before either of them could utter another word the server came back and placed the remaining of their order on the table along with his bill.

"So, where do we go from here?" She asked.

"Let's just start with this date and go from here."

Unbeknownst to Shelly, Paul had been following her since the day Antoinette was born. Awaiting for the moment his restraining order was null and void. Having to watch his only daughter grow up from a distance was the hardest thing he ever had to deal with in life. There were times when he was able to speak to her in public, was given the opportunity to hear her voice, and experience her smile on occasion. But, he was very careful not to make his presence obvious. No need of raising any concerns for stalking.

Over the years as Paul continued to watch both homes, he noticed

Shelly didn't have her life fully together either. He wondered what things would've been like for them if he had never asked her for an abortion. And now, because of his immaturity, it cost him the greatest moments of his life. He needed a plan and he needed one fast.

"How do you plan on introducing yourself to her?"

"I'm just going to walk up to her and introduce myself." Sitting in the passenger seat, watching Antoinette sip on a cup of tea, as she gazed into the morning sky.

"What!!!" Dramatically turning to face his partner in crime to be sure his ears wasn't playing tricks on him. "What you gone say?" He chuckled. "I's ya pappy." He continued to joke. "Nice to finally meet you!" He blurts out in laughter.

"For real man." Sucking his teeth. "What you think I should say?"

"Honestly." Looking over at Antoinette sitting at the table by herself. "I think you should tell her the truth."

Taking a deep breath. Paul opened the door and slowly placed his left foot on the pavement. His heart was racing and his mind was scrambling for peace. Nothing about this encounter felt right. But he knew it had to be done, because he was literally running out of time. Pulling back the chair adjacent hers. Paul cautiously sat down with a warm smile to greet her. Startled, by her guest. Antoinette hastily placed her mug down and reached for her napkin.

"Can I help you with something?" Staring her visitor innocently in his eyes.

"Umm…" Rubbing his sweaty palms up and down his outer thigh. "Yeah…" Sticking his left hand out to great hers. "My name is Paul Jefferies and I wanted to come over and introduce myself to you."

"That's real sweet of you." Refusing to shake his hand. "Paul is it?" Placing her napkin in her lap. "I don't do older men." With a 'kick rocks' grin on her face.

"Ha, ha, ha…." Paul snickered before he started to choke. Patting his chest with his fist. "I am not trying to push up on you sweetheart." Adjusting his ball cap.

"Then, what is it that you want?"

"Feisty, just like your mama."

"Excuse me?"

"I's ya pappy." Pulling his cap off to place it on his right knee.

Appalled, Antoinette stood from her seat. And before she excused herself from the table, she tossed the rest of the contents in her cup in his face and sashayed away.

"Jerk…"

Waiting until she was no longer in view, Bobby skipped over to accompany his friend and make light of his current position.

"Sooo…." Looking over the menu. "What happened?" Fighting the urge to laugh.

"You saw what happened." Placing his cap back on his crown.

"True, true." Motioning for the waiter. "I did see, but I didn't hear." Looking him over. "What did you say?"

"What you told me to say!"

"You didn't." With a look of surprise.

"What did you expect me to say?" Rubbing his hands across his face. "And close your mouth."

"Anything but 'I's ya pappy'! I can't believe you said that." Shaking his head in disbelief. "What did she say?"

"Nothing." Laughing as he replayed the image of the look on Antoinette's face after he admitted to being her father.

"So, what's your plan now?" Looking to see what's taking the waiter so long to come and take his order.

"Paying my old baby mama a visit."

CAT GOT YOUR TONGUE

Hearing the sound of cars passing as she attempted to rest on the bench beside the club. Tami tried to focus on what her next plan of action was going to be now that she was technically a free woman. She could be and do anything she wanted now, but the only thing she had to do was fake her own death. The only people that would know she is alive would be her brother and her crocket ass cousin, Lewis. Staging a death shouldn't be that hard considering all the money she had set aside for retirement, but she never would've thought she would've been retiring this early in the game. No one ever lives to tell the story of the hustle. But, maybe this time Tami would be the exception.

"Thank God for second chances." She whispers as the sun beamed down on her eyes. "I wonder if Arnez got my message." Lifting her aching body off the wooden bench. "I need to find a phone."

As Tami made her way to the front, she noticed a truck parked by the entrance. Unsure of who it could've been, she made her way through the door anyway. Assuming it may have been one of Arnez's employees coming to open up, she thought she'd step in and ask to use the telephone.

The door flung open and a shapely figure stood in the light. No words were needed, because he knew in his heart it was her. After everything he had been through these past three years. No one or nothing could change the joy and relief Arnez felt in his heart to see his sister alive and well. Beaten, bruised, and limp. He hopped up to embrace her with a warm hug that only a loving brother could give. And they wept.

"Boy am I glad to see you."

"I'm just grateful you're alive."

"Hell, I'm glad we're both still alive!" With her arms still wrapped around his neck. "Is everything ok?"

"Now it is," gripping her tighter. "I thought I was never going to see you again."

"I did to."

"Tell me what happened."

As Tami began to explain everything that took place that led up to her ending up in his club, Rock fumbled through his contacts to check to see why he hadn't heard from Nicole this week.

"What's up?"

"Hey."

"Why haven't I heard from you? Did I do something wrong?"

"No baby, everything is fine between us. I've been dealing with family issues lately. Where you at?"

"At Shelly's house watching the baby."

"Is Mike there?"

"Naw, just me and the baby."

"I'm on the way…"

Cameron hasn't answered her phone since the day she found Tami out in the yard. She'd been out of the loop for a minute, because she wanted to find a way to escape without being seen by her neighbor. A lot had transpired over the course of two days and she clearly wasn't thinking rationally anymore. Skimming through her missed calls, Cameron found she had six calls from Stephanie, eight calls from her mother, and one call from Reese. Unsure of who she wanted to call first, she placed her telephone on the counter and she scurried to pack her last bag.

"I got to get out of here." She plotted to herself. Taking one last look out her bedroom window to see if Bobby had come back home. Cameron grabbed her pup and made a break for the door, but to her surprise she had a visitor waiting on the other side.

"And where you running off to so early in the morning?"

"Boy!" Cameron shouted, squeezing the life out of Bear who was crying underneath her arm. "You scared the mess out of me!"

"I see." He chuckled. "Why you acting all antsy?" Admiring her frame as she brushes pass him with her head scarf on. "You look like you've seen a ghost or something."

"Look, I don't have time to sit and chat or whatever you came over here to do right now." Throwing her luggage in the passenger seat. "I got to go." Shoving her key in the ignition.

"Is everything okay?" Puzzled by Cameron's urgency to get started on her journey.

"I'll call you!" She yelled as she backed out of her driveway. Nothing was going to deter Cameron from making her escape. Not even a dick that she'd fantasized about for weeks, could force her to stay any longer. She had to go.

After having been driving for over an hour. Cameron never looked back to see if she was being followed. Knowing this was Stephanie and Ricardo's honeymoon weekend, it killed her to have to interrupt their special time, but she had nowhere else to go.

"Please, let them be here." She stated as she rang the doorbell, awaiting a response which seem as though it would never come. Stephanie slowly opened the oak wood door, still wearing her bridal gown, reeking of liquor, and looking as though she had been in a street brawl the night before.

"Damn, girl!" Cameron states, placing Bear down so he could run free. "What the heck happened to you?" Staring her friend square in the eye. But, Stephanie mumbled not one peep. She just stepped aside to allow her guest access to her dungeon of gloom. "Where's Rico? And, why it's so dark in here?" Looking around Stephanie's living room, wondering where all of the Champagne bottles came from. "Damn, girl." She laughed. "Looks like ya'll had a wild night."

"Tuhh!" Stephanie mumbled as she made her way back to the couch.

"Well, how did the wedding turn out?" Watching Step turn back another bottle. "Ain't it kind of early for you to still be celebrating?"

Suddenly, after hearing the toilet flush, Cameron heard footsteps coming in their direction. Preparing her congratulations praise, she was floored when she caught a glimpse of Step's guest.

"What the hell!" Feeling as though she'd been stabbed in the back.

(Ring, Ring, Ring.) Wondering who it could've been calling him so late in the evening, Reese reached for his phone that was face down on his night stand and placed it to his ear.

"Hello." Frustrated because the caller gave no response when he answered. "Hello!!!" Rolling over to his right side.

"Hello." A soft muffle came through the receiver.

Cracking his lids to see who it was that was disturbing his peace in the wee hours of the night. Reese's concern heightened when he realized it was Step crying on the other end of the line.

"Step, is that you?" Confused on why she would be crying on the eve of what supposed to be the happiest day of her life.

"Yes." She cried.

"What's wrong?" Finally able to focus on his surroundings. "I's everything okay?" Rising from underneath the covers. "Where's Rico?" Still awaiting an answer. "I'm on the way."

No matter what people had negative to say about Reese regarding his past life, one thing for sure, they could never down play the kind of friend he was when in despair. He was loyal to the end and no matter what the situation was, you can always count on him to come through. When Reese finally made it to Stephanie's and he saw her, she looked a hot mess. And, after she explained to him what all had transpired. He decided to stay the night because he was too drunk to drive himself home. They laughed, they cried, and they drank themselves to sleep until the doorbell rang and Cameron came barging threw the front door.

"It's not what you think." Reese exclaimed calmly.

"Well, somebody needs to start explaining something because this right here is foul." Folding her arms as she snapped her neck.

"Calm down man."

"What you mean calm down!" Getting louder as her anger festered.

"Dude left her at the altar." You could hear a rat fart in the room after Reese finished explaining his reasons for being at Stephanie's in the state he was in. "You would've known that if you would've answered your phone last night." He explained. "I even used her phone to call you, but not once did you answer or send a reply."

"I'm so sorry baby." She sympathized with Stephanie as she walked over to console her. "What happened?" Running her hands threw Step's hair. "You know what, never mind that. The past is the past. Let's get you out this house and get some food in your system."

Pulling into the diner, Cameron didn't notice Rico's cab parked in the lot because her attention was on finding a parking spot closest to the door. When they got out, Reese handed Stephanie a pair of sun glasses he found on the back seat to hide her puffy eyes. It was bad enough she didn't comb her hair, but he wanted to be sure no unwanted attention was drawn throughout their brunch.

"I hope they not to packed in here, because I'm starving." Cameron suggested as she pulled back the door, taking a seat in the nearest booth to the entrance, while motioning for the waitress as she made herself comfortable.

"Good morning." The server greeted as she laid their silverware on the table. "My name is Denise and I'll be your server today. What can I start you out with to drink?" Pulling her pad out of her apron.

"I'll have an orange juice."

"Let me get a coke." Reese requested.

"And, I'll have a water." Stephanie chimed in.

"Did you guys need a minute to look over the menu?"

"Yes, please." Cameron smiled gracefully.

"I'll be back with your beverages shortly." She stated as she made her way to the kitchen.

"The steak and cheese melt sounds real promising right now." Cameron chuckled as she contemplated on if she wanted to add the additional onions and mushrooms for thirty-five cents more. "What you got a taste for Step?"

"I don't feel like eating right now." She advised as the tears started to fall below her frames.

"Honey you got to eat something." Cameron argued. "I know you hurting and upset, but you've got to put some food on that stomach. Especially, with all the drinking you've been doing within these last twelve hours sweetie." Holding back her urge to cry. "Come on and order something. I got you covered."

As they continued to look over the menu. Reese excused himself from the table and went to use the restroom. Before he entered the stall, a man brushed passed him in a tuxedo brushing against him as he passed.

"Damn, bro." Reese confronted. "You're not going to say excuse me?"

"My apologies man." He exclaimed. "My mind was somewhere else." Shaking his head. "I'm sorry about that." Looking down at his shoes. "It's been a rough night."

"It's cool man." Brushing it off. "I hope everything works out for you."

"It's starting to." Rico smiled as he left the room. But his luck seem to have run out fairly quick because he was stopped in his tracks as he had to pass his ex-fiancé table to get to his own. Trying to think of a way to get past her without being noticed. Rico tried to hide his face behind a menu, but his efforts soon fail when the cashier asked him if he wanted to order to go aloud.

"Is that who I think it is?" Cameron questioned, directing her inquiry to no one in particular. Before Cameron had a chance to confirm whether her eyes were playing tricks on her or not. Stephanie had already risen and charged after him.

"Oh shit!" Cameron screamed.

"Somebody call 911!" One of the customers shouted as he made an effort to break up the one sided brawl. This definitely wasn't Stephanie's first time at the rodeo with having a physical altercation with Rico. However, this was the first time he never hit back.

"I'm sorry!!!" Is all you could hear from a defensive Rico and a 'You Bastard' is what you got repeatedly from Step. Eventually, they were able to break the two apart after him having received a black eye and a swollen bloody lip. But, you can believe she was still kicking at him as she was being carried away. After the crowd cleared. Mo was able to make her way from the back of the restaurant, but to her dismay, she saw it was Rico who had been attacked.

"Oh, my God!" She screamed. "Are you alright?" Throwing her arms around his neck. "What happened?" Trying to make eye contact through the swelling.

"BITCH!" Stephanie yelled as she tossed her shoe in their direction. And in that moment, Mo realized it was the woman he'd left standing at the alter in front of all those people, that opened up a can of whoop ass on her new man.

Fueled with anger, Cameron raced out of the parking lot in an attempt to escape before the authorities came and arrested them for assault and battery. Not only was she pissed because Rico had the audacity to be there. But, she was more angry at the fact that she didn't get her steak melt. It seems as though no matter where she turned, trouble seemed to be awaiting just around the bend. Wanting to make sure her friend was alright, she couldn't help but focus on her own ever present troubles as well.

"I don't mean to be insensitive or anything. But, I have to drop you guys off and head out."

"Are you freaking kidding me right now?" Stephanie cried. "You know what!" Resting her hands in her lap with a sudden calmness. "Go." She replies nonchalantly.

Reese didn't mumble a word. He knew better than to get in between a disagreement with friends. He felt bad for everything that transpired with Step. No one should ever have to experience what she went through. But his curiosity couldn't help but wonder what Cameron had going on as well.

She seemed a bit detached, but he didn't pry.

"Just text me and let me know you've made it to your destination." Acknowledging her decision to go.

"I will."

Ricardo was devastated. He couldn't believe of all the people he could've ran into and all of the diners, Step chose that one to come to. With her wound still fresh, he never intended on contacting her ever again in life. But, he guess God had other plans for him. Knowing what he did to her would scar her for eternity, but what he regretted the most about the encounter is the fact she saw him with another woman. Preferring she'd see him alone, but at least he didn't have to hide her any longer.

"Let's get out of here." Holding the bloody napkin to his lip as he picked up his blazer from the booth.

"Okay." She agreed. "Where we going?"

"To get a room." Walking gracefully out the front door. "I need some rest."

Danielle Walker

TRUTH BE TOLD

Fueled with rage, Antoinette rushed home, appalled by the encounter she experienced with the stranger. However, curiosity begun to sink in as she wondered what would motivate a man to approach her with accusations of being her father. Which was completely absurd, but a part of her felt as though there could be some truth in his revelation. Even though, she didn't give him an opportunity to chat long. She was taken aback when he first set down because of how much of a resemblance they shared. She played it cool and remained calm, but someone had some explaining to do. And she knew exactly where she was going to get her answers from.

Immediately after walking in the house, she noticed her mother had been cleaning because it smelt like Clorox and fresh pine. As she walked through the living room making her way to the kitchen Antoinette tossed her purse and keys on the sofa as she passed.

"Ma!" She yelled after over hearing the dishes.

"Yeah baby!" Searching for her pot she uses to make cornbread in. "I'm in the kitchen!"

Unsure of how she was going to ask her mother if the man she'd known to be her father her entire life was who they'd made her believe him to be or was it a possibility it could be someone else. Either way she focused on her breathing to prepare herself for the worst.

"Hey baby." Debra greeted as she welcomed Antoinette with a warm smile.

"Hey…" She dragged.

"Ow we," she stated as she began to mix her ingredients in the pot. "What's that all about?"

"You wouldn't believe the day I had." She sighed as she pulled back one of the bar stools.

"It can't be no worse than mine." She chuckled sarcastically. "Being I've been cleaning all day and now, standing here in this kitchen preparing supper." She implied while she measured the milk.

"The strangest thing happened to me today while I was having brunch." She began to explain as she kept her head down, fumbling with her hands.

"Well, what happened?" Debra asked as she whipped the contents of her bowl.

"A man approached me today and started making some strange accusations."

Immediately, Debra attention was zoned in on Antoinette and a rush of sweat started to form on her forehead. Anticipating the next part of their conversation.

"He stated he was my father."

The bowl shattered and the contents was oozing over Debra's feet. She feared the day she would have to explain to her grandchild that she was not her biological mother and everything she had been raised to believe was a lie. But, be it as it may, Paul had beaten her to the punch and there was no way of escaping the truth now.

"Mama, are you okay?" Concerned of why her mother would be so startled by her statement if it wasn't true. But, Debra said nothing. She stood there in complete silence as she stared her granddaughter eye to eye. "Are you okay?" Antoinette asks once more, realizing her mother had went into shock. Bending down to pick up the shattered pieces to assist with cleaning the mess, Debra finally exhales and begins to explain.

"It's true."

Lost for words, Antoinette felt like someone had taken a dagger and rammed it in her heart. The emotions that fell over her was something she had never experienced before. Wanting to know the details of what took place, she swallowed her pride and started asking questions.

"Why haven't any of you told me?" Wondering if her sisters knew Charlie wasn't her father.

"Well sweetie, Shelly was young back then and she wasn't ready to be a mother. So, I took on that responsibility and we raised you girls as sisters." Debra explained.

"What did you say?"

Realizing Paul never revealed the full details of their situation to Nette as she watched the tears began to fall from her face. Debra placed her hand over her mouth as she watched Antoinette run out of the kitchen.

"Antoinette!" Tossing the dish rag on the counter as she stumbled over one of the bar stools. "Let me explain!" But she was gone. Rushing over to the telephone to call Shelly and let her know what happened, Debra felt a sharp pain in her chest and fell to the floor before she had a chance to make the call.

Fueled with anger Antoinette rushed to Shelly's house going well over ninety miles an hour in a sixty-five speed zone. Unaware of the state patrol that had been sitting just a couple miles ahead clocking vehicles to meet his quota for the month. She sped right passed him and was later ordered to pull her vehicle over.

"Ma'am, did you know you were doing ninety-seven in a sixty-five speed zone?" Shining his flash light throughout the car.

"No, I didn't realize. I was just trying to get to my destination in a timely manner."

"I understand, but may I ask what's the hurry?" He asked as he continued to shine the light in the back seat.

"I just really have somewhere I need to be officer." She replied sarcastically.

"Ma'am, it's no reason for you to use that tone with me. I just asked you a simple question."

"Can you just write your little ticket so I can be on my way please." She snapped.

"You know what." Stepping back away from the door. "How about we finish this conversation down at the station." Placing his light back on his hoister. "Ma'am, can you step out of the car." He instructed.

"For what!" She argued as she refused to comply.

"Ma'am, I'm only going to ask you one last time before I have to use excessive force." Using his radio to call for back up.

"You ain't gon' do shit! I want my lawyer!"

Opening the door and reaching in to pull Antoinette out involuntarily caused her to fight back. Soon after back up arrived. Antoinette had been subdued and arrested for resisting arrest, reckless endangerment while operating a vehicle, and assault on a police officer. And, was booked with no bail until her hearing before a judge. Using her one call, she attempted to contact Debra but didn't get an answer because she was still lying in the floor. Therefore, she had to wait till morning before she could attempt another call.

Coming to the realization that life as she knew it was coming to an end faster than she expected it to, Shelly stared at the home she and Michael created and cried as she considered it was because of her they could never truly be happy. Attempting to clean her face before she entered, she looked around to make sure no one had been watching her because it felt as though someone had been following her. Stepping out the truck, making her way to the door, Shelly was stopped by the fear she felt strain on her heart due to the reflection staring at her from behind the window.

"We need to talk." He stated as he watched her body tremble. But Shelly said nothing due to the fear she had. "I want to see my daughter."

Wanting to protect the home she'd created. Shelly figured if she entertained the idea of Paul meeting Antoinette, than there'd be a slim possibility he'd go away. So she decided to play ball.

"I can't allow that to happen." She declined as she turned to face her past head on.

"You don't really have a choice in the matter anymore." He argued.

"Is that so?" She chuckled.

"It is."

"Well, why are you here telling me you want to see her if I had no control over what you do?" She questioned with a sly grin on her face.

"See, I already know everything I need to know about you and my little Antoinette, or should I refer to her as your sister Nette." He explains as she drew closer.

Stunned by his revelation, Shelly found it hard to digest how he knew so much about their living arrangements and he just came back in the picture.

"See, I know you may be puzzled on how I know all of your little secrets, but I have a secret of my own that I would like to share with you." Sliding his hand down the left side of her check. "I never left." Pulling her in for a kiss.

"Get your hands off of me!" Knocking his hands off of her and thrusting away to create space between them two. "Don't you ever put your hands on me ever again, you hear me! Or I'll have you locked up for assault." Adjusting her skirt as she attempted to ignore the sensation between her thighs. "I don't know what you're talking about, but let me make something crystal for you." Staring him in the ball of the eye. "Whatever you think you may know about me and my child is none of your business and if you ever come near me or her ever again. I promise you I'll kill you." She threatened.

"Really…" He laughed confusing Shelly by his amazement with her scare tactic. "Well, you may want to start arranging my funeral, because I spoke with her earlier today and she now knows who I am." Laughing as he headed to his vehicle. "It's high time we start discussing parental rights!" He yelled from his seat as he slammed the door. "I'll see you later on this week baby girl!"

Even though, Bobby gave Paul his word that he would stay and help him figure things out with Shelly and Antoinette, he couldn't help but think of a plan of how he was going to leave Georgia undetected. Now that the feds were involved he knew it was going to be even harder for him to pass the state line, let alone cross the border without his face plastered on every Most Wanted poster hanging at each checkpoint. He needed help and he knew the right person to call. Hoping there was still a chance they hadn't caught on to his trail.

"Yo."

"What's good man?" Surprised to see the name come over his caller ID. "I've been meaning to get at you. I need some extra cash real quick and I wanted to know if you had any work you could front me until I got back on my feet."

"Man.." Bobby replies in a distraught tone. "Honestly, things have been slow motion lately and right now I have bigger problems I need to solve or won't none of us be eating for a long time, ya dig." Rubbing his hand across his forehead.

"What's going on?" Giving Bobby his undivided attention.

"I need to lay low for a few days and I needed someone I knew I could trust and no one would suspect me ever being at their crib." He stressed. "Just a few days until the heat dies down and I can get a chance to hit the state line."

"Sure thing, sure thing." Peeping out his living room window. "You can crash at my crib for however long you need cuz. Just let me know when you plan on rolling through."

"Cool, cool. I'll be there in about an hour."

After hanging up with Bobby, Reese contemplated on what could've pressed Cameron to run off so quick today. It never occurred to him that she would leave her friend in her desperate time of need. Selfishness didn't fit her persona. At least, that's what he assumed about her. But, he knew whatever it was it had to be more than she was letting on and he was determined to get to the bottom of it.

Danielle Walker

WHEN IT ALL FALLS DOWN

Standing in the shower with her eyes closed, concentrating on the vibrations her body felt as the water covered her. Tami began to have flashbacks of when she was held captive in Bobby's home. Relieved that she had now been reunited with her brother and she was free, strangely a part of her wondered where Bobby was and if he knew she had escaped. Even though, he'd left her for dead, something about the way he took control when he had his way with her sent chills up her spine. She was curious of what could've become of them if the circumstances were different. Was he capable of love? Would he be as aggressive with his partner? Or, was this just a one-time act to put fear in her. Either way, she was hooked and she yearned for his touch.

Over the years Tami had her share of being promiscuous with men. In and out of situations is how she referred to them, because she felt she'd yet to find a man that could please her appetite or provide her with the love she dreamed of in her adolescent years.

"Where you at?" Orlando asked.

"At home watching t.v why?"

"Can you come pick me up and take me to my aunt house real quick?"

"Yeah."

Before Tamera pulled in the parking lot, she texted Orlando to let him know she was outside. After pulling in, she noticed him sitting on the curb with a duffle bag filled with clothes. After he settled in, they didn't utter one word the entire ride to his house.

"I want to marry you." He confessed before he got out.

Speechless and confused, Tamera continued to be silent. She turned and stared Orlando in the eyes with a look of sincerity on her face.

"You make a man want to get his act together. I'll even start playing golf and change the people I hang with for you. Whatever makes you happy I'm willing to do for you. All I know is I want you. I want us. Forever."

"Get out." She demanded with no explanation of why.

"Huh?" Shocked by her reaction.

"I have to go." Placing her foot on the break as she released the gear.

"But, I just asked you to marry me, Tamera." Placing his hand across his chest.

"I have to go."

Tami wanted a man that took charge. Made moves and made things happen. A provider. Someone who she could put her trust in that things would be handled and she didn't have to worry about where her next meal would come from or if she would have a roof over her head or not. A man she couldn't run over, but respected her to the utmost. Even though, on occasion he would have to put his foot down because she was getting too sassy.

"Is everything okay in there?" Arnez asked as he tapped on the door.

"Yeah, I'm okay."

"I'm going to order some pizza. Any special requests?"

"Pepperoni is fine with me."

"Alright, don't drown in there now." She laughed as he proceeded down the hall.

"Tuhh…" She chuckled. "He got jokes."

Finally stepping out onto the memory foam rug nearest the tub. Tamera kneeled to turn the knob but as she bent over, she remembered the moment she stared at Bobby as he showered while she contemplated stabbing him as he bathe. Startled, she shook off the image and cut the water off and started drying.

"I need to get out of this bathroom," picking up an additional towel to wrap around her head. "Pull it together Tami." She motivated herself as she stared at herself in the mirror. "You ain't in love." She laughed to herself, while she reached for the Colgate. Before she had an opportunity to place her toothbrush in her mouth. She threw up in the sink.

"Ohh…" She cried. "I really need to put something on my stomach. I hadn't ate in days." Scurrying to clean her mess and get dressed, Tamera noticed Arnez sitting in the living room.

"You look beat." She joked.

"You know it's hard out here for a pimp." Scrolling through the flight itinerary on his phone. "I'm booking us a flight to Brazil tonight. We can catch the nine o'clock to Florida and board from there at eleven thirty to paradise." With a look of satisfaction plastered over his face.

"What!" Shocked by the news of her brother plotting to get them out the country.

"We're leaving."

"What about your club?" Trying to find an excuse for them not to go.

"What about it?" Typing in his card information.

"So you're just going to pack up and leave everything you've built behind?"

"Hell yeah!" Frustrated with the thought of his sister questioning his decision making after everything they've lived through. "Time out."

Stopping in mid-type. "Wasn't it your plan in the beginning to skip town once things started turning south?"

"Yeah."

"Well, I don't know if you've noticed or not. But, the shit done hit the fan and we got to get the fuck out of dodge. On everything." He exclaimed. "Ain't nothing at that club but heartbreak and bad memories that I'm way passed being over with. He confessed. "I have more than enough saved for me to open another "Spot" in the Caribbean's or something." He argued. "As a matter of fact," placing his phone on the table. "I can leave the club to Rock to manage and he can wire me a fourth of what the club earns."

"What about family and friends?"

"I can make new friends!" He admitted. "And I know damn well you ain't talking about Lewis!" Trying to understand where her rebellion is stemming from. "You're the only family I need. You're the closest blood I got and I'm going to do everything I can to make sure you're safe."

Realizing there was nothing she could say to convince Arnez that they should stay. Tamera went ahead and agreed to them leaving the states that night. She figured with them gone. She wouldn't have to fake her death any longer and she wouldn't have to live constantly looking over her shoulder.

"Okay." She agreed. "But, I have to make a quick stop before I go." Picking up his Magnum keys on her way out the door.

"If you're not back by seven. Just meet me at the airport!" He yelled. "The flight leaves at nine.!"

Stephanie had been sitting on her sofa ever since she got home yesterday. Cameron was in such a hurry to leave and she couldn't ask Reese to stay another night to help her wallow in her pain. So she insisted he go home and get some rest. Therefore, she'd be left alone with her sorrow. Life as she knew it was over. The man she was supposed to marry, who she was settling for, left her at the altar. All the money she had saved over the past nine years had been wasted on a dress she was only going to wear once. And she was to ashamed to return to work and face the people that watched her get rejected on her wedding day. Therefore, in her mind she had nowhere else to turn. She wanted to be free. She wanted to go to a place in her mind where she could find peace and happiness and make her present a soon forgotten past.

Remembering the dealer she came across the night of the wedding. She searched her bra for the powder she had got from him and spread it on the end of the coffee table. He promised Stephanie this would her numb the pain. She had no prior experience with cocaine, but, she was willing to try anything that could make her forget the pain.

Closing the front door behind her, Shelly took a deep breath and released in relief. She feared Paul was going to not only do something to her, but she feared her family was now in danger as well. Pacing the foyer, she tried to think of a strategy on how she was going to deal with Paul, deal with Antoinette, and now deal with Michael who is now entangled in her drama due to her past coming back to haunt her.

"He can't ever learn the truth about my past." She whispered as she covered her mouth. Looking down at her watch, she didn't have much time before her husband got home. She needed to pack some clothes for the baby and she only had a good fifteen minutes to do so because he got home around six.

"Nicole!" She yelled out as she consciously tried to harbor her fear.

"We're in the baby's room!" She replied.

Jogging up the stairs. Shelly tried to think of something to tell Niko to convince her to leave.

"Have you spoken with Nette today?" She asked as she glanced around the room, trying not to make eye contact with Niko or Rock.

"Naa, I haven't heard from her all day." Picking one of the pacifiers up from the floor. "Can you go rinse this off for me?" Handing the binky to her boyfriend as a distraction to get him to leave the room, so Shelly wouldn't suspect anything happened between the two before she got there. "Why you ask?"

"I know I hadn't seen her today and she was supposed to text me and let me know if she was going to be able to baby sit for me tonight."

"Oh, naa. I ain't heard from her." Shaking her head. "But I'm about to head to the house real quick. If she's there, I'll tell her to call you."

"Thanks." Relieved Niko was about to leave without her having to trick her into leaving.

"No problem." She smiled. "We're about to go Rock, come on!" She yelled on her way down the stairs.

"I'll catch you later, Shell." He said as he passed her standing in the doorway.

"Lock the door behind you, if you don't mind."

"Sure thing."

As Rock was on his way out, Michael was on his way in. *'Thank you.'* He said as he closed the door behind himself.

"Baby!"

Startled by the sound of her husband's voice, Shelly rushed to lay the baby back down. "I'll be right down!" Trying to figure out what she was going to say. Before she could leave the room, Michael was staring her in the face. "Heeeyyyyy, baby." She greeted him with a smile.

"Hey there to you to sweet thang." Grabbing on her butt as he embraced her with a hug.

"We need to talk."

Michael had taken all he could take. Marrying Shelly was one of the happiest moments in his life, but ever since the day he put a ring on it, their lives have been one roller coaster ride after the other. He figured maybe this was karmas way of getting him back for marrying his best friends ex. But, he assumed by both of them being good people. They were deserving of one another. After hearing Shelly's truth. He decided they had come to the end of their road, because he couldn't handle dealing with another one of her crazy ex's. And he damn sure wasn't about to allow her to drag his son through it either. On May 7, 2016, Michael packed his bags and he left Shelly and took the baby with him. Realizing the mess her life had become, Shelly didn't put up a fight, because she knew this was the best decision for their family. And, she had to deal with her demons on her own.

"I hope one day when it's all said and done. We'd be able to reconcile our differences."

"If it be God's will, then maybe." He agreed. "If not, I hope you're able to fix the damage you've done to your family."

"Me too."

Finally, Cameron made it to her mother's. When she arrived her mom didn't ask any questions, because she knew Cameron only came home when she was in trouble. She just welcomed her back and asked her what kept her away so long this time around. Cameron had a history of leaving home for years and never coming back until something happened. Only because her family treated her like the black sheep. Nothing she'd ever done was good enough for them. She was always made to feel unworthy.

"Stop eating all that bread!" her grandmother shouted at her. "That's why you're big now!" Starring at Cameron with her hands on her hips. "Didn't you just eat a sandwich about an hour ago?"

"Yes."

"So, why are you in here making toast?"

"I was hungry again." She whimpered.

"Ain't nobody that darn hungry! I better not see you in this kitchen again!"

Are the memories she had of the traumatizing childhood she had coming up because her mom was a single parent and she worked ten hour shifts. Every morning Cameron was dropped off at her grandmother's house until her mom came and picked her up. She loved her mother with all of her heart. But, due to the fact that other family members verbally abused her. She taught herself how to become emotionally detached.

"Is it okay if I crash here for a few days?"

"Now you know, you don't have to ask permission to come home." Throwing her arms around her daughters neck. "Ernest coming over in a bit to pick me up." Taking the rollers out of her hair. "We're going to Biloxi for a couple days."

"What's a couple of days?" Rolling her luggage down the hall.

"Three maybe four days." Casually waving her hand around in the air. "Ernest get free rooms whenever we go." Combing her hands through her curls, while she structured her French roll.

"Okay," relieved that with Karen gone she could rest and not stress about being asked a million questions on why she'd come back home.

The view of her old room was so 90's. The pictures of her favorite models were still plastered on the walls. A calendar of puppies was hanging to the right. Her old television with knobs sat in the center. And to her left stood her five disk multi-changer radio and ceiling lamp. It had been years since she'd left and everything was the way she'd left it. Plus or minus a few cob webs.

Laying prostrate on her king sized comforter, Cameron cried herself in to a frenzy. Everything she'd worked hard for has now been taken away in less than a week after years of grinding. She knew the day she'd laid eyes on her neighbor he was trouble. The way he reacted to her coming over to introduce herself and welcome him into the neighborhood. The suspicious meeting he had in his front yard with those hoodlums. Even down to the way he kept watch of her house when he'd come out to take a smoke. He was trouble from the start. She cried and she cried, asking God why her.

Suddenly, she got it. Cameron refused to allow some stranger to come and run her away from the home she created for her and her pup. She loved her neighbors and the peacefulness of her neighborhood and she wasn't ready to give that up without a fight.

"If he wants a war." She said to herself as she wiped her snot on the pillow case. "I'll give him a war."

Danielle Walker

JACK OF ALL TRADES

After several attempts to reach Antoinette, Nicole decided to give up. She figured she may be having one of her infamous mood swings and she'd pop up sooner or later when she was ready to talk. Throwing her purse on the sofa, she picked up the remote and scrolled through the TV guide to see what kind of movies were playing that were worth watching. It had been a long day, let alone her energy levels were down to zero from all the lovemaking she and Rock did earlier that day. She forgot she hadn't eaten. Settling for 'The Lord of the Rings' marathon that was currently on FX. Nicole made her way into the kitchen where she found Debra lying in the floor with cornbread mix scattered all over her.

"MAMA!" She screamed, kneeling down to check for a pulse. She felt one beating, but it was very weak. However, it was a ray of hope and she knew if she didn't panic, her mother could be revived. Quickly dialing for an ambulance, Nicole jumped into survival mode. She gathered her and her mother's things so she would be prepared when the med team started asking her questions about insurance and picture ID. With little time to prepare, she figured she'd call Shelly on their way to the hospital.

The ambulance arrived at a quarter to seven. Nicole was standing in the doorway waiving to try and catch the drivers attention. With no time to spare, the medics were in and out within two shakes of a leg. Looking at the paramedics take care of her mom as they got her attached to a ventilator, Nicole reached for her phone to dial Shelly and inform her of where they were headed. But, before she had the chance to tell Shelly what had transpired.

"CODE BLUE!"

"Hello." Shelly answered. "Niko!" Looking down at her Nokia to make sure the call didn't drop. "Hello!" Placing the phone back to her ear, but all she could hear was this buzzing sound and then a loud thump.

"She gone. We've lost her." A man's voice came through the receiver. "Call it." He instructed the other medic.

"Six fifty-six p.m."

"HELLO!"

Waking up next to a man she hardly knew was a first for Monique. Never in a million years had it crossed her mind that she would be in love with a man that walked out of his wedding to be with her, without knowing anything about her. No matter how wrong it was morally, emotionally it felt right. Watching Ricardo sleep like a baby wrapped up in his tuxedo, brought a joy to her heart that she'd never experienced in her lifetime. She had been in love several times before, but this time around, she was sure she wasn't in love by herself. It wasn't long before he would wake and see her before she had a chance to freshen up. Therefore, Monique knew she had to get up and get a move on it before he got a chance to see her face unbeaten.

Walking into the bathroom, Mo stretched her body before she flicked on the lights. Frowning after tasting her morning breath, she reached for one of the complementary toothbrushes and proceeded with her morning routine. Wash face, brush teeth, put on lashes, and roll out make up. Arch eyebrows, draw eyebrows, and floss in between. Concealer, foundation, finishing powder, and blush. Eye shadow, lip pencil, lip stick, and gloss. She knew her limits and was trained not to overdo it. However, some days she'd put on just enough to where she'd look like another woman.

"Sex sells," her mother told her as she watched her get dressed for her date. "I'm not telling you to go out here and have sex with every man for money sweetie. All mama is trying to get you to understand is you have to use what you got to get what you want." As she smeared her red lip stain on her bottom lip. "Men are physical creatures and they consider beauty as what they can see," she explained. "Yeah, you hear those women out there telling you kids it's what's on the inside that counts." She chuckled. "But, baby," turning to look her daughter square in the eye. "I want you to listen to mama when I tell you, that ain't nothing but some b.s those insecure, self-righteous bitches, feeding you honey." Placing both hands on Monique's cheeks. "You hear me, baby?"

"Yes, ma'am."

"You understand what mama trying to tell you sweetheart?"

"Yes, ma'am."

"I want my baby to be happy. And, ain't no man going to want you looking like plain Jane. Okay?"

"Okay, mama."

"Every chance you get baby, if he has to get up and go to work at four o'clock in the morning." Putting her earrings in. "You need to be up at three o'clock getting yourself together." She warned. "Don't let that man catch you with rollers in your hair, or your face undone. Because he will leave, you can bet your bottom dollar he will. You understand?"

"Yes, ma'am." Admiring her mother as she watched her continue to dress.

"Mommy loves you and she only wants the best for you muffin."

Continuing with her mother's traditions. Mo continued to do what she had been trained to do. And that's to be breathtaking every time a man laid eyes on her. Putting on her finishing touches, Mo took one last look in the mirror and prayed this one stuck around for the long haul.

"Good morning." He greeted as he watched her enter the room.

"Good morning." She blushed, surprised that he'd awaken so soon.

"You're up pretty early."

"Yeah, I couldn't sleep." She lied as she took a seat next to him on the right side of the bed.

"You look amazing." He complimented as he brushed the hair back out of her face.

"This I know." She replies sarcastically with a snicker.

"Excuse se mua." He laughed. "What's on the agenda for today?" he asked taking in the thought that he may have made the right decision after all.

"How about we take things one step at a time."

"Okay, okay, I can handle that."

"Starting," she interrupted. "With you taking a shower and finding something else to put on besides that." Pinching her nose to insinuate the notion of his body odor being priority on their list of to do's.

"Alright." He agreed. "I'll clean myself up." Sitting up on the bed. "But, I thought you were supposed to love me for better or for worse."

"Last I checked neither one of us were married." She joked.

"Awe, shut up." Tossing a pillow in her face as he ran in the bathroom.

"My make-up!"

After Tami rushed out the door, Arnez knew he needed to make a few final arrangements before he closed up shop. 'The Spot' was a very lucrative business and his decision to part ways with his first baby was one of the hardest decisions he ever had to make up until this point. His decision to open up his first location in Atlanta, was the best thing that happened to him in a long time in a financial aspect. However, emotionally it has been a tremendous headache. From the death of the love of his life. To the moment where he almost lost his life in the middle of his parking lot. Parting ways with the club didn't seem like a bad idea after all. If he was going to leave everything behind. He knew it would only be fair if he left it to his most-trusted friend.

"Hey."

"What's good?"

"I needed to talk to you for a minute," Arnez advised.

"Sure thing, how are you holding up?"

"Everything's copasetic right now."

"How's Tami doing?"

"That's what I needed to speak with you about. Are you busy?"

"Na, I'm free right now. What you need?"

"Me and Tami leaving the country tonight. I've arranged us a flight to Brazil, but we're passing through Florida first and I don't know how long we're going to be gone."

"Word!"

"Yeah, something I felt was necessary for our survival, you feel me."

"I feel you," Agreeing with the decision Arnez decided to make. Even though it hurt him to see them go.

"Anyway, I'm leaving the club to you. It's yours completely. All I ask is that you wire me thirty percent of the earnings each month at the end of the period. I have plans to expand the brand."

"That's what's up man." Thrilled by the news. "I don't know how I could ever repay you."

"After all you've done for me. Helping out at the club, holding things down when I couldn't after Jasmine's death, and now this mess with Tamera, you don't owe me nothing bro." Reminiscing on all the times Rock had been there to support him without question. "You've earned it."

"I really appreciate this man," wiping the tears from his eyes. "You really don't know how much this means to me."

"Maybe now you can take Niko on a real date," he clowned.

"Man… Come on man." He laughed.

"I'm just talking shit man," he laughed. "But for real, I owe you everything. And this is just a small token of my appreciation."

"That's real G."

"My flight leaves at nine o'clock, so I'm about to head over to the club now to pick up a few things."

"Alright."

"I'll leave the keys under the dumpster in the back, beneath the left wheel."

"Bet." He smiled before he hung up. "Be safe out there in them foreign streets."

"Nah… I ain't got no worries."

Lewis received an anonymous text message advising him to meet at a secluded location by the dock where he and Tami did a fake bust a few years back. Assuming it was her and he was finally going to be able to have a face to face with her about the money she owed him, he hopped in his cop car and headed to the destination. Upon arrival he didn't see any cars in sight and he saw no sign of her either. After waiting patiently for another five minutes, he decided to text the number back and let her know he was there. Waiting for a response, he got a text of a smiling devil emoji and then he was surrounded by a bus full of Feds.

There was an anonymous tip called in to the tip line that a local APD officer had been trafficking drugs at the harbor and he was in possession of six keys in the trunk of his patrol unit. When he was ordered to get out of the vehicle with his hands up, Lewis advised he had reason to believe that something was going to happen there at their current location and he was there for the same reasons they were there. But when one of the officers ordered him to open his trunk, they found exactly what they were advised they'd find. There stood Lewis Crawford going down for drug possession he had no clue about. After he had been placed in the back of one of the other units, one of the deputies came over with a letter that he found in the back set of Lewis's car.

"Does this mean anything to you?"

'With love Tam'.

Danielle Walker

SURPRISE

After sitting around the house for the entire afternoon, Reese decided he would call and invite Cameron over for dinner so they'd have an opportunity to hash things out. He wanted to explain how he felt about her and try to make an effort to see if anything can become of their friendship. Bobby had already made himself at home in his guest room, but he knew he wouldn't be a problem due to he was trying to keep a low profile for the next few days. After texting Cameron his address, Reese proceeded to check in with his friend to make him aware company was coming.

"Hey."

"What's up?"

"I'm about to have a little shorty come through to chill for a minute," sticking his head through the door. "And, I just want to make you aware so you wouldn't be caught off guard when she got here."

"Na man, you're good," he chuckled. "Do your thing," scrolling through his social media on his mobile phone. "I'll lay low and take it easy in here until she leaves."

"Alright, I appreciate it bro."

"No problem, just make sure you make enough for me as well."

"I got you." Reese laughed before he closed the door behind him.

Pulling into the driveway, Cameron nerves were all over the place. She only agreed to come over to Reese's house for dinner because she felt bad for leaving him with Stephanie, and she needed something to help ease her mind about stressing over her own personal drama regarding her neighbor. Not only was she stressing over that, but she was concerned for her friend and her heartbreak as well. The least she could do was allow Reese to prepare dinner for her and show up as an effort to mend the fence. Taking one last look in the mirror to check and make sure her lip stain didn't smudge over her bottom lip, Cameron removed her keys from the ignition and proceeded to the door.

"Don't take your love away." Is what Reese was serenading before he heard the doorbell sound. *"Baby, don't take your love away from me I need you girl."* Tasting his sauce before he headed towards the door. Impatiently waiting, Cameron began to ring the bell nonstop. "I'm coming!" He yelled. *"I've been searching here and there, everywhere, and can't find no one like you girl."* He continued to say while opening the door.

"It's about darn time!" She greeted with an attitude as she brushed passed him.

"And, hello to you too!" He blushed.

"What took you so long to answer the door?" Turning to face him with her hands planted on her hips. "Good grief!"

"I was tasting the sauce."

"The sauce?"

"Yes!" He chuckled. "The sauce." He said heading back into the kitchen with his apron in hand and Camron on his heel.

"Look at you," she smiled. "Trying to be all romantic and junk." Flopping down on one of the bar stools. "What are you cooking anyway?"

"Spinach lasagna with garlic bread on the side."

"Umm, that sounds great."

"It is…"

"I'll be the judge of that," she flirted.

After setting the table for them both, Reese placed a beautiful decadent dish in front of Camron for her enjoyment, before he placed his down as well.

"Bon appetite."

"Umm, this look amazing," admiring the healthy portion he placed on her dish.

"Well." Finally taking his seat. "I really hope you enjoy it."

"I'm sure I will."

Before Cameron had an opportunity to savor her meal., she was distracted by the creeping of an opening door.

"Don't be alarmed." Reese advised. "A dear friend of mine is visiting me for a few days."

"Oh…" Letting her guard down as she took another bite of her meal.

As the footsteps drew near to where they were seated, Cameron was curious as to who this friend could be and if it was a guy or a girl, Reese never specified. Now that the mysterious individual was in plain view, Cameron spewed her food all over the dining room table. Reese didn't know what was going on. However, he knew something was going on between her and Bobby due to the fact that she was holding a butter knife aggressively in her right hand. Of all the people she could have ran into, she never would've thought Bobby would be the one coming out of Reese's back room.

"YOU BITCH!" Bobby screamed.

TO BE CONTINUED

ABOUT THE AUTHOR

Born and raised in Atlanta, Georgia. Danielle Walker has always strived to become an entrepreneur since the early age of eight. It started with odd jobs around the house, which soon led to braiding hair for extra cash. Becoming a Corporate Lawyer has always been a dream of hers, but it soon changed in her early semesters of college. Where she had the opportunity to intern for one of Atlanta's most prestigious law firms 'The Mosby Law Group'.

Seeing and experiencing firsthand the hectic-ness of running a law firm. Danielle decided that particular career field wasn't for her. Continuing to work two jobs and maintain being a full-time student. Danielle eventually realized working extremely hard wasn't something she wanted to do either. Later she found herself at a crossroad because she didn't have a plan B.

With life experiences having their way with her and her motivation to make something of herself at its peak. Danielle picked up her pen and did what she felt came natural to her. Today Ms. Walker is the owner of 'YJLM Publishing House' and is the author of one of the bestselling books of 2014. Optimistic for the future, you can guarantee she is ready to take on her next challenge in life. One day at a time.

www.ingramcontent.com/pod-product-compliance
Lightning Source LLC
Chambersburg PA
CBHW030538180626
46810CB00005B/1924